AF481781

# A Fun Bedtime Story

## For Boys

Lastesha Roberson

Timmy is at school but he isn't feeling so well.

Timmy lost his first tooth yesterday and still is a bit upset.

The front desk calls for Timmy because his mom is here to pick him up. He makes sure he doesn't leave his favorite toy truck.

He is sad. Timmy always have so much fun at school.

"Are you feeling okay buddy?"
says Timmy's mom
"Yes could we go get ice cream
pleaseeee mom?" he begs
Of course buddy
ice cream it is.

"Yay! I want chocolate ice cream mom" Timmy yells
Timmy mom orders him chocolate ice cream in hopes it would cheer him up
ICE - CREAM

"I'm happy to see you in a better mood little guy. How about one more stop before we head home" his mom says

Timmy is so excited to see where his mom is taking him

On the way to the new location Timmy's mom tells him to close his eyes because it's a surprise.

When Timmy opens his eyes and
sees the park his face fills with joy
and excitement.

Little Timmy is so happy,
he gives his mom a big giant hug.

Timmy is having fun. As he runs through the playground when suddenly falls and hurts his knee.

"Owwwww mommy it hurts" He cries out.

As Timmys mom gets up to see what's wrong, another little boy sees Timmy hurt.

Zack runs over to Timmy. He helps Timmy up because he sees him hurt.

As Timmy's mom runs over she sees that Timmy is not crying anymore and asks if he is okay.

Timmys mom smiles as she grabs her emergency kit and puts a bandage on his knee.

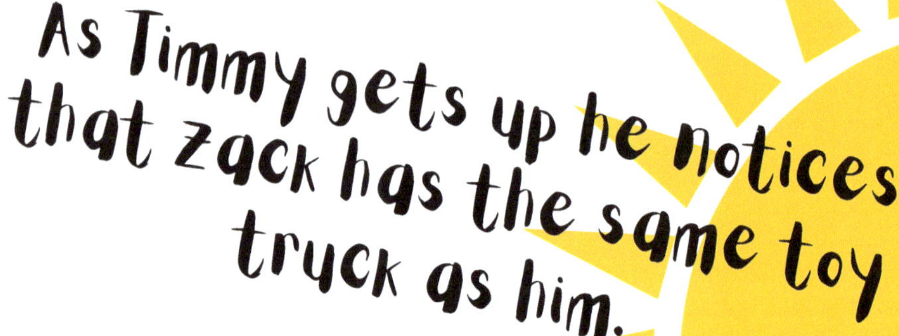



With the sun still high in the sky, Zack asks Timmy if he wants to play. Timmy says yes and they both race to the swings.

. They play on the swings,
laugh on the seesaw and
take turns sliding their favorite
toy truck down the slide.

As the sun sets the little boys sadly say goodbye to each other and go home.
Bye Zack !
See you later !

Timmy moms asks "How are you feeling buddy, did you have fun?"

"Yes yes yes" Timmy says. He immediately asks if they could visit the park again tomorrow.

# The End